J Braun
Braun, Eric, 1971-
How to outsmart a martian /
$8.99   on1051777649

How to Outsmart a Martian

WITHDRAWN

Eric Braun

BLACK RABBIT BOOKS

Hi Jinx is published by Black Rabbit Books
P.O. Box 3263, Mankato, Minnesota, 56002.
www.blackrabbitbooks.com
Copyright © 2020 Black Rabbit Books

Jen Besel, editor; Michael Sellner, designer;
Omay Ayres, photo researcher

All rights reserved. No part of this book may
be reproduced in any form without written
permission from the publisher.

Library of Congress Cataloging-in-Publication Data
Title: How to outsmart a martian / by Eric Braun.
Description: Mankato, Minnesota : Black Rabbit Books,
[2020] | Series: Hi Jinx. How to outsmart ... | Includes
bibliographical references and index.
Identifiers: LCCN 2018015189 (print) | LCCN 2018043644
(ebook) | ISBN 9781680729283 (e-book) | ISBN
9781680729221 (library binding) | ISBN 9781644660591
(paperback)
Subjects: LCSH: Flatulence—Juvenile humor.
Classification: LCC PN6231.F55 (ebook) | LCC PN6231.F55 F45
2020 (print) | DDC 818/.602—dc23
LC record available at https://lccn.loc.gov/2018015189

Printed in China. 1/19

Image Credits

Alamy: Marco Lachmann-Anke, 6–7 (ship); Dreamstime: Isaac Marzioli, 19 (boy); Sofia Santos, 14–15 (alien); iStock: memoangeles, Cover, 10–11 (Martian); Shutterstock: Alexandra Petruk, 7 (alien); bastetamon, 13 (alien); brgfx, 4 (bkgd), 16–17 (pond); Christos Georghiou, 11 (t), 12 (torn paper); cylnone, 3, 7, 21 (bkgd); ekler, 9 (torn paper); Freestyle_stock_photo, Cover (bkgd), 12 (bkgd); Igor Zakowski, 16–17 (alien); karavai, 14–15 (bkgd); KennyK.com, 19 (milkshake); Lorelyn Medina, 19 (cone); Memo Angeles, 4–5 (kids & birds), 6, 12–13 (cow, pig, & grass), 16–17 (kids), 19 (alien & brain), 23 (cow & pig); NoPainNoGain, Cover (chemistry bkgd); OK-SANA, 16–17 (bkgd); opicobello, 12–13 (torn paper); Pasko Maksim, Back Cover, 17, 23, 24 (torn paper); pitju, 10, 18, 21 (curled paper); Refluo, 14–15 (mosquitoes); Ron Dale, 5, 9, 14, 20 (marker stroke); rwgusev, 4 (UFOs); Sarawut Padungkwan, 1 (bl & br), 12–13 (Martian), 23 (alien); shockfactor.de, 20; Silviya Skachkova, 2–3, 8, 21 (eyes); Stockway, 8 (bkgd & Earth); sundatoon, 1 (boy); VectorBar, 11 (b)
Every effort has been made to contact copyright holders for material reproduced in this book. Any omissions will be rectified in subsequent printings if notice is given to the publisher.

Contents

CHAPTER 1
Greetings, Earthling...5

CHAPTER 2
Know Your Enemy....9

CHAPTER 3
Outsmarting a Martian...............14

CHAPTER 4
Get in on the Hi Jinx..20

Other Resources............22

Chapter 1
Greetings, Earthling

Imagine this. You're at the park. All of a sudden, someone starts screaming. "The martians are coming! The martians are coming!" Flying saucers race across the sky. Kids and parents start to **panic** in the streets.

You stand alone in the road as people run past. Everyone is screaming. You're scared too. But you can't help it. You want to get a look.

Prepare Yourself

Crunch! A flying saucer lands, crushing your school. (Sad, I know!) A ramp lowers, and a dark figure comes out.

Stop right there. If you've ever seen a movie, you know this could happen. You might have to deal with aliens at any time. And that's why you have to know how to outsmart them.

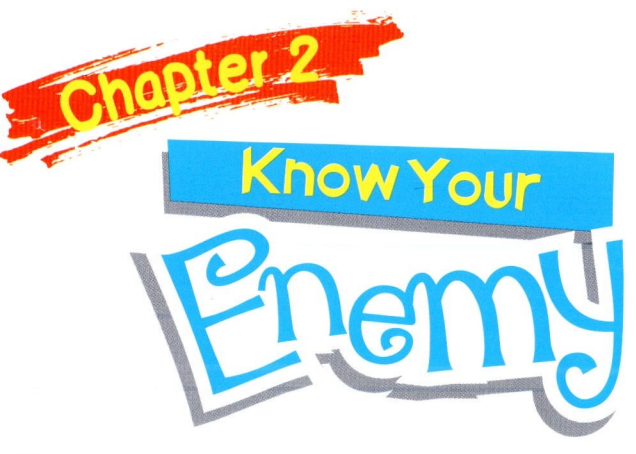

Chapter 2
Know Your Enemy

To outsmart a martian, you have to know what makes it ooze. (It's not blood.) The trouble is, we don't know a lot about aliens. We don't even know if they **exist**. That's because other planets are far away from Earth.

Other planets are really, really far away. At its closest, Mars is more than 34 million miles (55 million kilometers) away. And it's one of the nearest planets!

Check the Tech

We do know one thing. If aliens traveled all the way to Earth, they have great technology. Super-fast spaceships. Highly advanced power sources. Incredible computers. And they for sure have super-zappy ray guns. If you're going to travel to distant planets, you have to be able to **defend** yourself.

Different Kinds

Books and movies make it pretty clear there are two main kinds of martians. The little green men are a common **variety**. They usually have big foreheads. The other alien type is tentacle creatures. Their slimy **limbs** flap around. This is cool to look at. But don't get wrapped up.

Chapter 3
Outsmarting a Martian

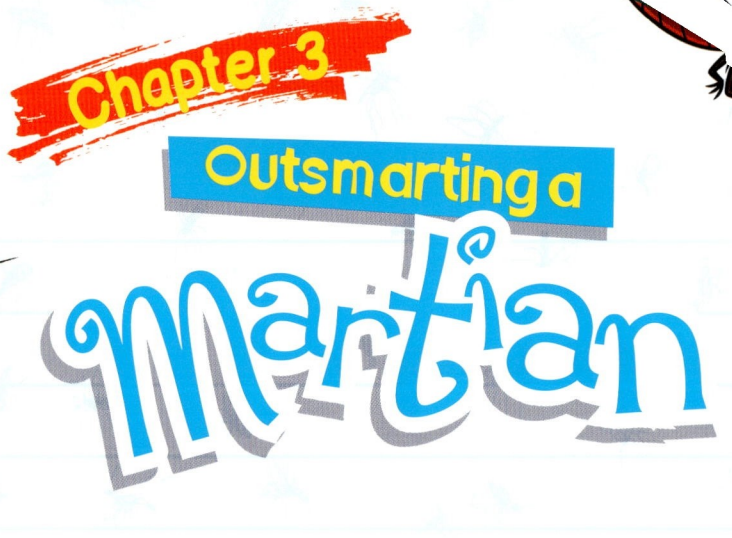

Now let's talk about ways to stop these creatures. Start by thanking the martian for saving you. Explain that the mosquitoes are in charge. Say they use humans as **slaves**. The martians will go after the mosquitoes, not you. Bonus—no more mosquitoes!

Tip

It's not nice to tell the aliens your principal is in charge. Stick with mosquitoes.

Dealing with the Tentacles

Are you facing a tentacle creature? Go onto a frozen lake or ice rink. The martian will slip and slide all over. It will have no control, and you can push it around. Wheeeeee!

Another great idea is to cook up some squid. Eat the seafood—tentacles and all. The tentacle martian will flee in horror. And you get a yummy snack!

Dealing with the Green Guys

Maybe you're facing a little green man. Remember those large foreheads? A big forehead means a big brain. So feed them lots of ice cream and smoothies. Tell them to eat fast. (They will love it!) Then sit back and watch as their big brains get big brain freeze.

Aliens might be tricky. But so are you! With these tips, you're ready to stop any aliens that get in your way.

Chapter 4
Get in on the Hijinx

Of course humans don't know if aliens will come to destroy Earth. But it is fun to think about defeating one in person.

However, people are on the lookout for aliens. Every year, many people report **unidentified** flying objects (UFOs). Some ranchers say aliens kill their cattle. The animals do not have a single drop of blood left.

Maybe the aliens are already here.

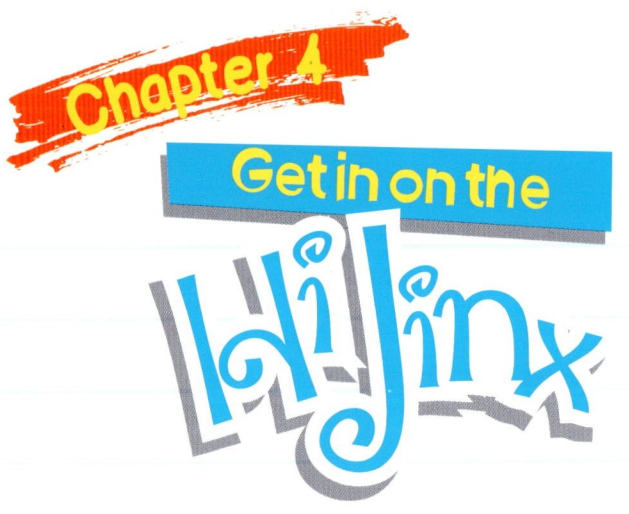

Take It One Step More

1. Do you believe other planets have life? Why or why not?

2. Imagine humans find a way to visit other planets, such as Mars. Would you go for a visit? Why or why not?

3. Many stories about alien visitors show them as unfriendly. Why do you think that is?

GLOSSARY

defend (de-FEND)—to fight in order to keep something

exist (ig-ZIST)—to be real or have life

limb (LYM)—the leg or arm of a creature

panic (PAH-nik)—to have sudden overpowering fright

slave (SLAYV)—someone who is owned by another person and forced to do work without pay

unidentified (un-i-DEN-ti-fiyd)—not able to know who someone is or what something is

variety (vuh-RI-uh-tee)—something differing from others of the same general kind

BOOKS

Coddington, Andrew. *Aliens, UFOs, and Unexplained Encounters.* Paranormal Investigations. New York: Cavendish Square, 2018.

Murray, Laura K. *Aliens.* Are They Real? Mankato, MN: Creative Education/Creative Paperbacks, 2017.

Terp, Gail. *The Search for New Planets.* Deep Space Discovery. Mankato, MN: Black Rabbit Books, 2019.

WEBSITES

Life Beyond Earth
sciencenewsforstudents.org/article/life-beyond-earth

Life on Extrasolar Planets
www.esa.int/esaKIDSen/SEMXWOSTGOF_LifeinSpace_0.html

The Search for Life
nasa.gov/content/the-search-for-life

23

A

alien invasions, 5, 6, 20

L

little green men, 13, 18

M

Mars, 9

P

planets, 9

S

stopping Martians, 14, 16–17, 18

T

technology, 10

tentacle creatures, 13, 16–17

U

UFOs, 20

W

weapons, 10